For
Tom Deering
who came with
his bears
M.W.

For Sarah
P.D.

First published 1994 by
Walker Books Ltd, 87 Vauxhall Walk, London SE11 5HJ

10 9 8 7 6 5 4 3 2

Text © 1994 Martin Waddell   Illustrations © 1994 Penny Dale

This book has been typeset in Stempel Schneidler.

Printed in Hong Kong

British Library Cataloguing in Publication Data. A catalogue record for
this book is available from the British Library.

ISBN 0-7445-2569-1

When the Teddy Bears Came

Martin Waddell ◆ Illustrated by Penny Dale

WALKER BOOKS
AND SUBSIDIARIES
LONDON ◆ BOSTON ◆ SYDNEY

When the new baby came to Tom's house,
the teddy bears started coming.

Alice Bear came in the cot.

Tom kissed Alice Bear and the baby.

Ozzie Bear came with Uncle Jack.

Ozzie Bear had a flag and a hat.

Ozzie Bear sat on a chair,

where he could look after the baby.

Then Miss Wilkins came with Sam Bear
in his sailor suit. Sam Bear sat on the chair
beside Ozzie Bear.

"*I* want to give our baby a bear!" Tom said.
So he gave the new baby his Huggy.
Tom told Mum, "Huggy can look after
our baby now."
Tom put Huggy beside Alice Bear.

Rockwell and Dudley Bear came in a van.

They were squashed a bit.

Tom unsquashed them for the new baby.

Rockwell and Dudley Bear went on the chair

beside Ozzie Bear and Sam Bear.

Gran brought Bodger Bear from her attic.
"That's my Bodger Bear!" Dad said.

Mum said, "Look at our baby with all of these bears!"

Tom looked at the bears. Alice Bear, Ozzie Bear, Sam Bear and Huggy, Rockwell and Dudley Bear and Dad's Bodger Bear, all on the couch beside Mum and the baby.

"There's no room for *me*," Tom said to Mum.

Mum smiled and said, "Come here, Tom, and sit on my knee. You and I can look after the bears. It's Dad's turn to look after the baby."

And that's what they did.
When the new baby
came to Tom's house
they all took it in turns
to look after the bears ...

and all together they looked after the baby.